THE ADVENTURES OF COBASFANG

GOOBELLA'S ACCENT

(Volume 4)

BY: DAVID E WALKER

THE ADVENTURES OF
COBASFANG

GOOBELLA'S ACCENT

Coloring Book

(Volume 4)

Copyright © 2025 by David E Walker

ISBN 978-1-7375821-8-2 (Paperback)
ISBN 978-1-7375821-9-9 (Digital)

All rights reserved. No part of this book may be reproduced or transmitted in any form or by any means without written permission from the author, David E Walker.

For permissions contact:
David E Walker
W-Thing Publishing LLC.
8201 Harford Road #10941
Parkville MD 21234
or at www.cobasfang.com

Printed in The United States of America

THE ADVENTURES OF COBASFANG

JUSTICE RETURNS
(Volume 1)

RAID ON NORGON CITY
(Volume 2)

WAR OF THREE REALMS
(Volume 3)

GOOBELLA'S ACCENT
(Volume 4)

THE AWAKENING
(Volume 5)

Visit cobasfang.com for incredible SWAG

&

Coloring Books Too

www.ingramcontent.com/pod-product-compliance
Lightning Source LLC
LaVergne TN
LVHW081548060526
838200LV00048B/2258